Angel's Angels and Fairies

The Art of Egle "Angel" Wierenga

Stories and poems by Ray Wenck

Stories

Egle "Angel" Wierenga is a full time artist.

As a child growing up in Lithuania, she had a passion for light, color, fantasy and symbolic expression. Her love of animals, nature, and a human form, always has her trying to find beauty in the surroundings. Never short of inspiration, sometimes she feels it is a race against time to produce all of the images in my mind.

She graduated from Applied Art Technical Institute, in Lithuania, where she studied fashion design and different techniques in art. After graduation, she worked as a custom fashion designer in several design salons in Lithuania.

She came to United States in 1999, and since then has been residing in Orlando, Florida. Her husband, Daniel, has been her biggest supporter through her most difficult times, and now he is her biggest help with printing production, merchandise and all the events that they travel to and attend together each year.

She has been sharing her artwork throughout the United States and around the world, for more than 15 years and continues her journey as a POP artist today.

You can find her artwork at *PIQ Gifts and gallery, Universal City Walk, Orlando, FL,* or you can catch her at Convention Events, that are listed on her website at EWArtwork.com

Ray Wenck taught elementary school for 35 years. He was also the chef/owner of DeSimone's Italian restaurant for more than 25 years. After retiring he became a lead cook for Hollywood Casinos and the kitchen manager for the Toledo Mud Hens AAA baseball team. Now he spends most of his time writing, doing book tours and meeting old and new fans and friends around the country.

Ray is the author of twenty-eight novels including the Amazon Top 20 post-apocalyptic, Random Survival series, the paranormal thriller, Ghost of a Chance, the mystery/suspense Danny Roth series and the choose your own adventure, Pick-A-Path: Apocalypse series. A list of his other novels can be viewed at raywenck.com.

His hobbies include reading, hiking, cooking, baseball and playing the harmonica.

He first met Angel at a comic con where her and husband Dan had an impressive display of artwork. He was intrigued by the piece entitled depicting an angel and demon playing a game of chess. He envisioned them playing for a soul and a story, then an idea came to life. This volume is the fruit of that first seed of inspiration.

Angel of Peace

Angel of Peace

There will be peace. But it starts with you. If you can't find or feel peace, how can you expect it to grow? Make it your goal, your dream, a wish for mankind. Let there be peace. Yes, peace in our time. Be patient zero. Spread the idea one person at a time. We can do this. We can make a difference. But it starts with you. Be the change you want to see. Peace be with you.

Peace be with you, I do declare.
It is a wish, but perhaps more a dare.
A seed that grows from earth and air
Nurtured to ripe with hope and prayer.

It's what you seek, or so you say,
At any price, your will to pay.
Yet anger and hate rule your day
While love and joy are pushed away.

I challenge you to find your peace.
Discover joy, renew your lease
on a soul that is light and free.
Let anger loose and hatred cease.

You have the power to make change
Start with you then expand the range
Spread peace 'til it's no longer strange
Enjoy a new life, now rearranged

Go forth, rejoice, and spread the word
Peace is the way, it must be heard
Spirit take flight, soar like a bird
Free and uplifting can't be weird.

So, say it with me, say it true
To old friends and so many new.
A heartfelt wish and a prayer, too.
A blessing I give, peace to you

Universal Love

TWO

Universal Love
Forbidden Love

"But, where shall we go?" she asked. "Where in this world is there a place so accepting as to allow us the freedom to love who we choose?"

He gave her that confident and knowing smile. "The place exists, my love. It has to. How could it not? How could God bring us together, only to deny us? He is not a cruel master, but a loving Lord. He would not have given blessing to our love if we were not allowed to be together."

"But what if He has?"

"I refuse to believe that. I trust in my faith. To think otherwise is to deny His existence. We are destined to love if only to give birth to acceptance."

She turned to him now and took in his beauty. Not only his physical perfection, but the glowing ball of warmth that was his soul. How could she not love him? She placed her hands on his face and held him. Not moving. Not speaking. Just gazing deeply into his eyes and basking in his positive energy.

His pale eyes sparkled with light from a thousand stars. His alabaster skin was radiant. She could feel…no that wasn't quite right…she absorbed his being through her hands. It helped keep her spirit high. Her faith wasn't as strong as his, and she feared so much. But his positive nature was a perfect balance for her negative energy and self-doubt.

They had been chased from every land they had settled in. None had acceptance in their hearts, only hatred in their souls. If they were not like them, there was no place in their communities. But love, true all-encompassing love could not be wrong. She had to believe, to hope that a future existed somewhere.

Why couldn't the people they encountered see the love that bound them together? How could they not understand that basic need, that urgent desire, to be with the mate of your choosing? It felt so right. How could anything so beautiful be shunned so viciously?

Yet, here they were. Locked in a barred room. Imprisoned for their love and their differences. Waiting to stand before a magistrate to plead their case.

And what was that case? Love? Was it love that was on trial? Her will weakened and she knew he could see it in her eyes, on her face, and deep within her heart.

"You must have faith, my love. But if your doubts are too strong to see this through, I will understand. Only speak the words and I'm sure you can be forgiven, perhaps even accepted again."

The horror of his words struck her like a physical blow. She reeled. Her legs went soft and she feared she was about to faint. But as always, he was there for her. Holding her up, keeping her from falling.

"How-how could you say that? Do you not think my love to be as strong as yours?"

He smiled, but no warmth found his eyes. Only a profound sadness filled the orbs.

"My love, I don't doubt your love. I fear that love will be your doom. I do not wish that for you. You waver, but I understand that, for fear is a constant nag for my attention as well. But for you, there is an alternative; a salvation. Do not deny that you have not given it the thought it deserves. You can free yourself from this situation. You can still live."

"Yes, it's true. I have entertained the notion of casting you aside for my own survival, but what kind of life would I have, knowing I rejected my one true love? No, giving you up is not an option. We will face this together."

"And what if they find against us? You understand what that means."

"I do. But they will be the damned, not us. No, my love, if I cannot live with you, I will die with you."

He held her close, brushing a gentle kiss across her forehead.

The rattle of the key fitting the lock drew their attention. Before the door swung open and their final embrace ended, he leaned lower and whispered, "My heart is yours always."

Her eyes filled. "And I love you, as well." Their lips touched in a kiss so gentle and full of love as to transcend the Earth to a more spiritual plane.

They were ushered up a dimly-lit stone stairway into the bright light of morning sun. As they were led outside, a hush descended over the assembled townsfolk. They were paraded through a gauntlet of soldiers to a dais, where the local lord and his prim and proper wife sat.

The royals eyed them with contempt and disdain, giving them a strong indication of what the trial outcome would be.

"You have been brought here to stand trial for the most indecent and immoral affront to God as I have ever born witness to," the lord of the land said. "Your sinful relationship is-is…it is just wrong."

"In whose eyes is it wrong?" the defendant said, interrupting the lord.

"Why, in God's eyes."

"And who are you to presume how God sees us?"

The man sputtered, spittle flying as he tried to answer through his indignation.

Before he could speak, the defendant continued. "It's more likely to be in your eyes that you see our love as wrong. But who are you to judge? Are you God?" Again, he continued before the man could respond. "I see no God. I see a man who thinks he is better than others and has no true understanding of what love is."

A guard stepped forward and drove the flat side a halberd across the man's back, driving him to his knees. His love screamed, wanting to go to him, but her arms were held behind her, preventing her from moving. With a grunt of pain, he pushed to a standing position and lifted his head in a prideful and defiant manner.

The lord stood, glaring down at him. "I find you guilty before God of immoral behavior and relations with this woman. I sentence you to burn at the stake until dead."

"It's so easy for you to condemn that which you are incapable of understanding," his love said. "You've probably never loved anyone but yourself. If you haven't loved as completely as we have then how can you pretend to sit in judgment? You know nothing of us, but because we're different, you allow your petty fears to cause you to destroy rather than try to understand and accept. You are heartless and have a black soul."

The crowd shouted, drowning her voice, but from the faces of many, she saw she planted doubt. A woman locked eyes with her and gave a nod. She got it, but she would never speak up in support, knowing the fate imposed on her.

The lord held up his hands for quiet. Although silence did not return, the volume lessened enough for him to be heard. "You are a woman. One of us. If you swear before God that you were coerced into this relationship, perhaps had a spell cast over you, you may be pardoned for your sins. How do you plead?"

She ceased her struggled against the hands that held her and glanced around. Many of the anxious faces showed fear for her. They wanted her to repent, to deny the love she professed and return to the fold. In that moment, she faltered.

"I-I, uh..."

She cast a guilty glance at her beloved. He smiled. "It's all right, my love. Save yourself."

Her eyes filled and spilled huge tears. She shook her head. "No. No. I will not give you up."

His smile grew wide and warm.

"Then have faith. We will be all right and we will be together. I promise."

And with those words and the calm, confident demeanor he displayed, she turned to the arrogant lord and proclaimed, "I love this man with my entire being. His fate shall be mine and I feel sorry for those who have never felt love as deeply as this, to lay down your life to be eternally together."

"So be it," the lord said with a note of disappointment. "I sentence both of you to be burned at the stake."

They were pulled toward a stake already prepared with wood and kindling. Men bound them to the wooden pole that jutted skyward from the center of the pyre.

Though fighting with all her strength, she was unable to prevent the whimpering. As the men advanced with the torches, waiting

for the word to be given to light the fire, he turned around to look at her.

"Do you trust me?"

She swallowed hard. "Y-yes."

"I promise you will feel no pain. Do you believe me?"

The words were spoken with such confidence. An inner calm filled her like the holy spirit. All doubt fled her then, replaced by a feeling of pure euphoria. "Yes. I believe you. And I believe we will be together forever."

"Good. I love you."

"And I you."

The command was given. The flames touched dry kindling and ignited. The torches were tossed onto the larger cuts of wood. The flames grew taller. The heat rose and surrounded her. Despite her resolve to do otherwise, fear licked at her like the flames.

As the searing heat became unbearable, she felt the ropes that bound her go slack. She stared down at her freed hands, unsure of what to do. She could leap from the fire, perhaps only receiving minor burns. Instead, she wanted to free her love. She whirled to set about loosening his bonds, only to find him facing her with the most heartwarming and loving smile she had ever witnessed.

"Your faith and your heart have saved you. I told you to trust me."

She stared uncomprehending. Over his shoulders were the heads of pure white stallions, each with large feathery wings. He wrapped her in his arms and the wings encircled them in a bubble. The heat did not penetrate.

"Hold on," he said as the clear globe with the white wings surrounding it rose into the air.

Over her shoulder she said, "Always."

They were lifted skyward, human woman and Centaur man, and drifted with the wind currents. They rose above Earth's atmosphere and soared to the heavens.

She thought they were dead. Had died and risen to heaven, but it did not matter. She was wrapped in her man's loving arms and they had eternity. After what felt like a lifetime later, they began a long, slow descent, landing in a valley of plush green. They settled and the wings retracted, dissipating the bubble. The stallions bent to their knees in a bow and sped off to join a herd. In the distances she spied a village with assorted beings in residence. Astounded, she looked up.

"What is this place?"

"I told you a place existed for us."

"Is this heaven?"

"As close to it as can be. Come."

She walked with him toward the village. She did not know how he managed this strange and wondrous world, but she did not care. They were together and around people who accepted them. A place where they could live together eternally.

Soul of the Earth

THREE

Soul of the Earth

Mother Earth

I see you, my children. I see what you've done. I roam my creation and see the abuse you have caused. It was my gift to you; a blessing bestowed and look how you have treated my world. You insult me with your careless handling of this planet. How dare you destroy such a wondrous creation, this beautiful Earth. I will not stand for this betrayal.

I gave you all you needed to live, but you always want more. Your pollution, your drilling, your waste, and your bombs continue to weaken the fragile balance I have established for you. You chip away at the very thing that supports your ability to live. Are you a race of fools?

The boundless waters for drinking and the seas teaming with various food supplies are being poisoned. They are dying a slow but steady death. When they are gone, the peoples of this world will destroy each other for the last remaining drops until they, too, no longer exist.

The lands have been stripped and contaminated to the point they no longer sustain trees, foliage, or crops. The infected land produces food that further contaminates the once-abundant wildlife, which in turn has a long-term poisonous effect on you. Your greed and lack of respect for the environment has created a dangerous sustenance circle that contributes to your demise. Though once partaken for fuel, your own delicate internal balance has been thrown off, but the food supplies, you grow and breed. It now works to dethrone you as the superior beings on this world. Your bodies are in open rebellion against you, riddling you with diseases that fast outrace cures.

Even the air, once so light and crisp and pure, now invades you like a virus, stripping you of energy and vitality, leaving you with infested hulls. You perish at younger ages than you should and yet it need not be.

The population has exploded and is on a path of self-destruction by sheer numbers. My creation was never intended to support the number of inhabitants it now hosts. That must change and I have the power to enable solutions.

I am disillusioned by your lack of awareness of the problems you have caused. But I will not allow you to wreak ultimate devastation upon my world without retribution. This Earth will live on long after your race has ceded its domination. I have already taken measures to ensure my survival, for indeed my existence is tied to the life of this planet. If I am willing to fight to save this planet for my existence, shouldn't you be willing to do the same?

I have unleashed a multitude of low-level earthquakes, a record number of tornadoes, hurricanes of such raw power as to drive deep inland and purge the land of its overabundance. Volcanoes have begun to build their pressure, ready to explode and spew their molten streams and deadly ash-filled clouds over these lands. Tidal waves have risen to titanic heights, washing the lands clean, readying them for a rebirth.

All of these and more will I release upon you until you see the folly of your ways. We will either come to an agreement to restore that delicate balance that sustains us all, or you will be wiped from this beautiful creation of mine. You are but lessees on this planet, and as landlord, I hold the right to evict. I will no longer tolerate your abuses. I will eradicate you and turn the world over to creatures and species who will respect the gift I have given them.

Enough is enough, my children. Please. Come to your senses now, before it is too late. Heed me, children. Heed me, I beg. For only you have the power to save this world for future generations of humankind. If not, well, I have the power to end humankind.

The choice is yours.

Healing Angel

FOUR

Healing Angel

To thee, I offer healing,
To thee, I do grant peace.
There is no greater feeling,
when hatred is released.

To look upon your brothers,
and sisters of this world.
With love for one another,
your heart flag now unfurled.

So, stand with me united,
in a dream for all mankind.
That we can be far-sighted,
and find peace within our time.

Devil and Angel Playing Chess

FIVE

Devil and Angel Playing Chess
Playing for a Soul

She was startled to see her counterpart already there. Usually, she was first on the scene when a soul was near collection. She knew this one might be close but held out hope that in the end, this soul would be coming with her. The expression on Doronda's face told Angelina she was surprised, too. Angelina stopped short of the dark realm where her counterpart dwelled.

"Why are you here?" She rolled her head back to one side, then forward, leading with her chin, displaying her usual attitude. "There's no debate as to which side this one will fall."

"No?" she said in an airy voice, trailing off with a faint hint of amusement.

Doronda eyed her with contempt and a trace of suspicion. "What game are you playing, Angelina? Are you disputing our claim?"

She shrugged. "I just go where they send me."

"Yeah. Right. Miss All Pure and Innocent."

"Let's just say this one may come down to a coin toss."

Doronda tilted her head back and barked out a deep, harsh laugh. "If you think you're going to waltz in and steal her from me, you're in for a fight. You have no business here. Unless, of course, you're so hard up for new recruits you're lowering your standards."

Angelina made no response. She made a sweeping motion with her hand and the veil swished aside like wind blowing a fog. She looked down at the hospital bed and studied the woman. The once vibrant woman was in a coma, the only signs of life made by machines. Angelina's boss would have to grant a miracle for the woman to survive, and one wasn't coming.

She mentally reviewed the file she'd been presented with earlier. Debbie Elizabeth Cramer. Thirty-six. Unmarried. Mother of two—a five-year-old boy, Dylan, and a three-year-old girl, Madison. She worked in a floral shop inside the local grocery store by day and bartended part time in the evenings at a local biker hangout. She lived with her mother and the kids in a two-bedroom apartment. By all accounts, she appeared to be a good mother but often had difficult relationships. Many of her boyfriends led her astray, as was the case with the most current one.

Arthur "Motor Head" Jenkins was a motorcycle mechanic. He lived fast and loose, often ending up on the wrong side of the law. He'd served several two-year terms for assorted infractions and couldn't seem to stay rehabilitated. He enjoyed the rush and convinced Debbie to take part in his most recent endeavor, the robbery of a drug rep, and things went bad fast.

They managed to pull the woman over to the side of the road. When Arthur opened her sample bag, all he found were packs of boner pills and respiratory tablets.

"Where's the Oxy, bitch?"

"We don't carry Oxy anymore," the woman said with a shaky voice. "With all the overdoses and the government crack downs, the company decided to cut it from our inventory." She sobbed. "I'm sorry. Take whatever you want. Just, please, don't hurt me."

Arthur knocked her down and tore the car apart. His rage grew by the second until he turned from the car, roared into the night sky, and kicked the woman in her head. Despite Debbie's protestations, he lifted his leg to stomp down on her head. Before the blow was delivered, blue lights flashed.

The police car barreled toward them. Arthur jumped into the car and screamed. "Go! Go! Go!"

Debbie floored the pedal and the chase was on. She vowed this was the last time. She was tired of dating losers. She said a silent prayer for the woman.

Unfortunately for her, the chase only lasted a minute. At an intersection they collided with a pickup truck, sending the unbuckled Arthur through the windshield and to his death.

Debbie smashed her chest into the steering wheel. The airbag failed to deploy.

She coded on the scene but was resuscitated. In the hospital she went in and out of consciousness. She was rushed to surgery, but the surgeon held little hope for recovery. The drug rep was in critical condition. Debbie was an accessory to the crime, and most likely looking at jail time if she recovered.

Her mother arrived and sat with her, hands folded, lips moving in a silent prayer. A short time later, a doctor and hospital administrator came in to discuss the situation. Debbie's mother cried, long after they left.

Debbie had done some bad things, especially in her wild youth. Angelina wondered why she was here. It wasn't a clear cut and dried case. It could go either way, but soul collectors like her were only sent when a soul was in doubt. In her mind, Debbie was leaning in the opposite direction. Unless something had been withheld, which was entirely possible, Angelina felt this was a lost effort.

She switched her gaze to her counterpart. Though always angry, Doronda had an ethereal, dark beauty. Long, thick red hair flowed from her horned head, draping over her blue skin. She was long and lithe. Her fingers extended into claw-like fingers. The reddish leathery wings were folded behind her as she paced. She whirled and opened her mouth to speak, then changed her mind.

She sat in her realm; dark, stormy, and foreboding. Angelina shuddered. If only the living could see what the choices for eternal rest were, the world would be a much nicer and happier place.

Angelina smiled seeing the pile of skulls next to Doronda. She always traveled with the skulls of those she fought with when they realized their eternal destination. It amazed her to see the lengths the dead went to avoid the dark realm. If they'd put that much effort into doing the right thing, they wouldn't be put in that position. In the end, Doronda always got her soul. Perhaps the skulls made her feel better about herself, knowing others suffered as badly as she did.

Angelina's side of eternity was bright and vibrant; the colors lighter and happier. Her own feathery wings unfurled, soaking in the warmth and peace. She closed her eyes and basked in the light. Flowers sprouted around her, yellow and fragrant. Where Doronda's world was dark and rough like a cave, her world displayed greenery and mountains. Beauty surrounded her in every direction. She felt sorry for those who would never get to see eternity as she did.

She studied Doronda. She actually appeared nervous about the situation. There was always the potential for a fight between collectors, should the soul be a toss-up. Angelina had won the previous six confrontations. Doronda didn't want to lose to her again. Her boss could be very cruel to those who failed him.

An idea struck. "I'll tell you what…"

Doronda huffed. "This oughta be good. Go ahead. Tell me what?" She made air quotes around what.

Angelina smiled at her lack of trust. "I'll play you for Debbie's soul."

"Debbie?"

Angelina frowned and pointed downward with the tip of a wing.

Doronda glanced down. "Oh, is that her name?"

"You don't know?"

"I don't care. Once she's with me, her name no longer matters."

Angelina mulled that over for a moment, then said, "So, shall we play for her?"

Doronda's eyebrows shot up. "Seriously?" Whatever she expected Angelina to say, it wasn't a game challenge. It piqued her interest, if not her curiosity.

"Go on."

"You're a semi-intelligent creature. Let's play a game of intelligence."

"You've got to be kidding me? Why would I do that? She's clearly, on my side of the board."

"Not from where I'm sitting. If she was already lost, I wouldn't have been sent to collect her. There is doubt somewhere. Even you have to admit that. This one is still in question."

"Have you seen her most recent exploits? That alone is enough to send her to me."

"And yet, here I am. You should do a deeper search when taking a soul to get a picture of their entire life, not just the most recent."

"Blah! Blah! Bleh! Save the goody-goody lectures for someone who cares."

"I'm sorry you're so unhappy in your chosen profession. It's too bad they don't have do-overs. I'd be willing to bet you'd do things differently, wouldn't you?"

"Who says I'm unhappy? I love my job."

"Okay. Then in the interest of keeping this sporting, I'll play you for Debbie's soul."

Doronda's eyes narrowed with strong suspicion. "You're up to something."

"Not really. We might be sitting vigil for a long time. Rather than have both of us wait, we'll play a game. The loser leaves. Simple as that. Both of us won't be wasting time. Just the winner."

Doronda thought about that. "And what kind of game are you suggesting?"

Though she already had one in mind, she pretended to think about the choice. If she spoke too soon, Doronda might suspect Angelina had a scheme to steal another soul.

Moments later, Doronda said, "Okay. I accept, providing we can agree on a game and you're not stacking the deck."

"Cross my heart and, well, you know." Angelina gracefully motioned as she spoke.

Doronda snorted. "I suppose you have a game in mind?"

"I do. Chess."

Doronda pursed her lips as she pondered. "How do you propose we play when we can't cross to each other's plane?"

"No problem. We'll place the board midway between planes. Half in light, half dark. If at any time a move must be made on the opposite side, we'll turn the board the other way."

Again, Doronda pursed her lips and scrunched her face. She looked more like she was constipated instead of thinking. She glanced down at the hospital room. Nothing had changed. Switching her gaze, she caught Angelina's eyes and bored into them.

Angelina's expression was neutral and calm.

"This is a trick. I can feel it."

"No. It's not. But I understand how you might feel that way. After all, it was your realm that brought lying and trickery into the equation."

Doronda nodded slowly. "All right. I accept the challenge. Winner take all. But if I catch so much of a scent of a double-cross, you and I will go to war. Understood?"

Angelina offered a smile at the empty threat. "Understood." Although spirits and already long dead, it was possible to destroy a soul. To do so took an extraordinary amount of power and the support of the realm's hierarchy. An offended party was able to do significant harm to the opposition but did not have the power or authority to end a soul.

With the snap of her long dainty fingers, Angelina made a chess board appear and float a foot off the ground equidistant across the spiritual line of scrimmage. Appropriately, black was across from her. Angelina folded her legs underneath her long, flowing translucent skirt. Her lightweight wings glowed outstretched at her sides. She brushed long blonde hair over her shoulders. "White goes first."

"Of course. Stupid rule."

Angelina moved her pawn two spaces. Doronda countered.

"What happens if we end in a draw?" Doronda said

"Then we'll switch to something more suited to your mental prowess, like tic-tac-toe or rock, paper, scissors."

Doronda paused with her fingers above her next move and glared at Angelina.

"Stumped already?" Angelina said in a mocking tone.

"Bitch!" Doronda said and completed her move.

The game went on for a time. Since they no longer walked the physical world, time held little meaning. They locked eyes and concentrated on the board, neither willing to give the other an opening. Winning was paramount and overshadowed their purpose for being there.

Angelina took a pawn. Doronda captured a knight and Angelina countered, knocking out a second pawn.

Their concentration was so complete that it was only by accident Angelina caught movement in the hospital room. As they hovered above, the monitor displayed a flatline. Debbie was gone, though the staff had begun resuscitation protocols. Angelina didn't want to get caught staring, so averted her gaze just as Doronda gave a smug look and flashed confident smile.

Angelina pushed her face closer to the board. She had not seen the last move. It took a few seconds before she found it and the reason for Doronda's smugness. She switched the board side, trying to scan from the opposite side. She needed to drag the game out a little longer.

She placed the board back where it was and smiled to herself. In her overconfidence, Doronda had missed something. Angelina would have checkmate in three or four moves, depending on Doronda's counters. She made the first of them, taking a bishop and leaving an opening for Doronda's rook to place her in check.

Angelina could feel her opponent's excitement radiate across the board. She sneaked another long glance at the lost soul. It floated above the body in search of a direction, but did she have reason to believe Debbie belonged in her realm?

Doronda made her move. "Check." The smile spreading across her face was triumphant.

Angelina knitted her brows and sucked in her lower lip. Again she turned the board and made the second move, blocking the rook's path and creating a dilemma for Doronda. "Check," she said, her voice syrupy sweet.

Doronda frowned, the tips of her horns glowing red. She studied the move and the situation. She was forced to move to protect the king, but she'd lose the rook. Whether she saw it or not, would be in checkmate one move later.

While Doronda tried to find a way out, Angelina watched the events below. The doctor made the call. Debbie was officially deceased. Medical personnel were with Debbie's mother. A tall woman in a business suit spoke to her, then showed a series of papers on a clipboard.

Debbie's mother placed a hand to her face. She flushed, looked at her daughter's body, then squeezed her lifeless hand. She stepped back as two transporters entered, unlocked the bed, and wheeled it out in a hurry. The doctors followed. The administrator shook the mother's hand and left.

The woman sat alone and smiled through her tears. She looked to the heavens. As the prayer filtered into her being, Angelina knew the direction the soul was going.

Doronda made her counter. The cocky smile was gone. She had seen the end and knew it was over. Angelina picked up the appropriate piece and moved it in the opposite direction of the checkmate. Doronda was too shocked to prevent her mouth from gaping. She glanced from the board to Angelina and back to the pieces. She leaned forward, searching for the trap that had to be there.

When she slid her queen into checkmate position, she looked up triumphantly. However, Angelina was no longer there.

Angelina swooped down, called to Debbie's soul, and led her to the light, warm, and happy realm. The organ donation had been the swaying factor. Her unselfish gift had helped others to live. Now Debbie's soul would reside for eternity in peace.

Angelina wished she could've seen the look on Doronda's face when she saw that she and Debbie were gone. Her anger would rage within her until the next time they faced off. But she would deal with that when the time came. For now, she, Debbie, and the realm were winners.

Angel's Prayer

SIX

Angel's Prayer
An Angel's Prayer for Humanity

From this perch I watch, as I have always done,
since the dawn of time and the birth of the sun.
I saw you crawl, stand erect, walk, then run
facing challenges; some you lost, some you won.

With each generation you grew and advanced,
learning skills; some developed, many by chance.
You worked hard, discovered play, embraced romance,
found your voice, raised it in song, created dance.

Through good, through bad, you emerged and moved ahead,
riding waves of elation, fighting past dread.
Throughout history, it could always be said,
you lived, you loved, you learned, but is love now dead?

I watch with sorrow as the hatred does grow.
With each passing day, I see a horror show.
Anger, mistrust, greed, lust and lies, don't you know,
work to deal humanity a death blow.

What should the color of one's skin have to do
with the soul inside and the love that is true?
For love is the answer, the spiritual glue,
that holds us together and creates us anew.

What's so wrong with caring and living in peace?
Is it so hard to share instead of, 'first me'?
Our egos have cast us alone on the sea,
adrift, and lost, but it's not too late to see.

Rekindle your love, embrace your compassion;
it's never too late for positive action.
Take that first step and mend if but a fraction.
Treat others with kindness, let peace get traction,

I beseech thee all, lovely children of Earth,
cast off your hate and rage; give love a rebirth.
Do not wait for others, open your heart first.
Let the light from your eyes shine love, peace, and mirth.

It's not too late to break the binds that hold me,
if they ensnare me complete, you cease to be.
For I am love, peace, faith of humanity.
This course you've set, brings the end, can't you see?

You are the hope, the future of you and me.

Beauty of Time

SEVEN

Beauty of Time

Time

I am Time's mistress. I have spent eternity watching as worlds evolve until their eventual and inevitable destruction. I have witnessed the passing of countless planets, stars, and universes, but what holds a sad and aching part of my soul is the loss of so many races, cultures, and civilizations. I have seen and known them all. I keep a piece of them alive within me as evidence of their existence.

The sentient and intelligent beings who have inhabited the known universe have all battled and lost to the same invading army: time. If I could reach out and speak to the current life forms, perhaps the third from the sun, or maybe the one with the four moons in the next universe, I would implore them, give thanks to the time they have and set about to fill those moments with as much purpose as possible.

Live fully. Embrace all. Love much. Let your spirit soar and your soul feel complete. The saying, *Time is short* is as much an understatement as to say it is never ending. It is impossible for the mind to engulf the full extent of eternity. I have existed for that time, and it slips even me.

Existing life does not comprehend. Time is a gift, but they see it as a curse; something they must fight against. To stretch as long as possible. But from the moment of their birth...no, of their conception...they are chained to this world by time. Whether for a second, a minute, an hour, day, week, month, or years, they will remain enslaved to time.

The weight of time cracks worlds, alters landscapes, and determines how life evolves. It is ruled by nothing. The universe, the planets, moons and stars, and every other particle is affected by time. Nothing is immune to its power. Man has decided his version of time's length, but it is fluid and never changing—neither slowing nor speeding. It just is. And no power in existence, past or future, can control it.

Perhaps the gods or God, or whatever the current religious belief beings hold above them has some say in time, but even they cannot cease its advance. It is eternal as long as the universe exists. But even then, who is to say it does not continue to progress though no being has life and the mental capacity to understand or track its passing?

It is sad they just don't accept the gift and live each moment with joy and enthusiasm. To spend their lives worrying that *Time waits for no man* is as inane as believing *Time is on your side*. The inevitability of their time ending is foregone. Once accepted, they break the binds of fear-limited life that holds them immobile to their plodding journey to life's end. Only when free of those chains can they begin to truly live the life they have been granted.

I beseech you, one and all, to embrace the finite time you have and enjoy each moment as if it were your last, because as sure as time passes, it may be.

Rejoice.

Live.

Your time spent will be well worth the time given.

Hummingbird Fairy

EIGHT

Hummingbird Fairy

Fairy of the Forest

Gleenda hovered twenty feet above the hummingbird, smiled, and watched as it flitted from blue flower to white flower. She loved to watch them. So fast, so beautiful, so fragile. Its purple and blue wings beat so fast against its green breast as to create its own unique blend of color and sound. Just like all of the wild and plant life of this tropical forest. She often dropped in to observe her creatures. So much beauty abounded here. So much joy and peace.

As the hummingbird darted off, she focused on a dainty and vividly colored butterfly. Its wings flicked against the slight breeze, then ceased to allow it to float. It lit on a petal, pulling its bright blue wings in tight to its slim, dark body. It swayed in the breeze, a perfect complement to the luminous white flower.

A large snail made its way beneath the green carpet of the intertwining vines on the forest floor. Her own feathery, yet powerful green, yellow, and blue wings melded with the natural backdrop of the forest. She slowed their beats to allow herself to drift lower. Her delicate fingers moved the greenery aside and smiled at the snail's pitifully poky pace. Extending a long finger in front of the snail, she coaxed it to climb into

her hand. She floated upward, lighting on a branch. The snail crept along her arm.

"Hello, my little friend. How has your day been?" Gleenda turned an ear and lowered her head. She laughed. "A little slow. Oh, you are too funny." Her green eyes sparkled with joy. "And where would you like to be?" Again she listened "Wherever the food is hiding. I can help with that." She drifted downward, flying inches from the ground. "What? Oh, here?" She set the snail down next to a large rock half buried in the ground. "Good hunting," she said, and flew upward in search of more interesting creatures. Their voices filled the forest from every direction. It was a symphony to her pointy ears.

Gleenda swooped low, scooping up an armful of small flowers. She sat on a low branch and peeled a thin vine from the trunk of an old tree. Humming softly, she set about threading the flowers onto the vine. The first was small. She was pleased with the end result. She set it around her neck, adjusted it for length, then tied it off.

Glancing down, she enjoyed its beauty against her pale skin. "I think I'll make another." This creation was long enough to wrap around her slim waist. She stood on the branch, her small frame barely bending the bough, and swirled to watch her new creation spin around her. She danced and laughed.

A thunderous boom interrupted her performance. The entire forest went silent and shivered in fear. She spun in a complete circle to determine the direction. A loud continuous roaring filled the trees. It was a sound unlike she had ever heard. She was sure of one thing. It was not the voice of a creature who belonged here.

The hummingbird blurred past, circled her twice, then hovered near the side of her head. Gleenda tilted her head to listen. "Destroying the trees? What do you mean?" She listened more. "And they just knocked the trees down?" She looked up as another loud boom reverberated through the forest. "We cannot allow this to continue."

With uncharacteristic speed, Gleenda flew toward the invaders. She reached the edge of the forest surprisingly sooner than anticipated. She hovered above the trees and watched in stunned silence. An entire section of the majestic trees lay scattered on the ground like so many corpses. Discarded as if they held no importance. Their lives snuffed out for no purpose.

Who were these invaders? These killers; mass murders. This intrusion, this grievous affront to their peaceful world must end. She glanced around before realizing that if her forest was to be saved, its salvation was on her slim shoulders.

Gleenda allowed the anger to boil within her until she could no longer contain her actions. She dove straight at the lead beast, a large smoke-spitting creature with a massive steel shovel on its face. It tore into a smaller tree. One barely two decades old—a baby—and ripped it from Mother Earth.

As it toppled toward the ground, Gleenda whizzed past the beast's rider and kicked him in the face. He screamed and flailed at her. Staggered, the rider released its hold on the beast and it ceased its assault on her beloved trees.

Her attack wasn't fatal, but it did give her information. The beast did not move without the rider to control it. She dove in for another attack. The rider swung his head toward her. His eyes widened, seeing her approach. Gleenda shifted her body to lead with her feet and drove them straight into the rider's face with all the force her eighteen-inch body could muster.

His body was propelled from its berth on the beast and toppled to the ground. Gleenda lit on a branch to watch. The rider rose, blood covering its face. He pointed at Gleenda, shouted, "Diablo!" and took off running toward the others like him. Other beasts came to a stop as their riders converged on their injured companion. He gesticulated wildly in Gleenda's direction.

Some of the rider's looked her way. Others laughed. Then, as a group, they advanced toward her. They stopped twenty yards from her perch. Though she couldn't understand their words, she saw they were agitated. They studied her. Several called out to her. Gleenda wished she could understand them. Some of her sisters did. They insisted she prepare for the battle to come, but she had ignored their warnings about the brutal attacks on their homelands. She had not taken them seriously, doubting the truth of their reports.

She had been wrong.

One of the riders lifted an object and pointed it at her. A sharp crack came from the item and something plowed into the branch inches from her body. Startled, she flew from the branch and hovered near the trunk.

The invaders gasped and pointed. Their chatter was loud as everyone spoke at once. Several of them made strange designs across their bodies with their hands. Two turned and ran. The remaining invaders spread out and kept pointing toward her. Not knowing what they were doing made her feel panic. For the first time in her life, Gleenda felt afraid.

Another crack and something ripped past her, fast enough to hear it whiz. The buzz reminded her of the bees that inhabited the forest, only this moved so much faster. She touched her face where the buzzing creature passed. It burned.

Fear wrapped its ugly arms around her. The man with the strange cracking thing pointed it at her again. She dodged behind a tree trunk as another crack sounded. Something burrowed into the tree.

"Forgive me, ancient one," she said to the tree. "I did not mean to bring you harm."

Caught between fear, guilt, and anger, Gleenda poked her head around the tree. The invaders moved closer. They spread out, trying to locate her. She soared to the top of the tree, then flew deeper into the woods.

Gleenda reentered the forest from above, landing on a branch. No sooner had she landed than a flock of birds surrounded her, all squeaking and whistling at once. "Quiet, my dears." They gradually fell silent. "It appears our home is under attack. It is nothing I have ever seen or dealt with before. I am not sure how best to handle this, but I fear if something isn't done, we will have no home left."

That started a wilder cacophony. Many birds flew off, too afraid to hear more. Others joined them, including other forms of life. Spider and howler monkeys crawled down from the trees. A large anaconda hung low over the branches. A red-eyed tree frog perched next to her.

Gleenda looked at all the confused and frightened creatures. Most she had known their entire lives. This was a danger far beyond the natural order of the jungle. Within this realm, a natural balance kept life teeming. But this was an alien invasion that threatened not just that balance, but their extinction.

"We have to stop them. Now. Before they forge too deep into our home. Go, my friends. Spread the word. We make a stand."

None moved. Then several toucans and a macaw took flight, and the exodus began. An excitement ran through the trees. But this one was far beyond the norm. This current was born of fear.

Gleenda raced to the forest's edge. As she arrived, the roar of the beast erupted to greet her. She stopped behind a tree and peeked out. The rider was back in its seat, readying the beast to continue its assault. Other invaders stood around the beast, scanning the trees. Searching for her. Several carried the cracking things and pointed them up into the trees.

A distant roar drew her attention. Three more beasts moved toward the first one to join in the attack. "Oh, no!" Gleenda had to do something. But what? She dove to ground level and searched for a weapon. She found a stone and a stick. She hefted the stick.

It did not have much weight. The damage would be minimal. An idea struck. Maybe it didn't have to be heavy.

Using the stone, she scraped and pounded one end until it had a point. She scraped it against the rock to sharpen the tip. Taking the stone and her small wooden spear, Gleenda set off to save her forest.

She flew to the far right of the last invader. He was twenty feet from the tree line. The sound of the other beasts was louder. They were close now. The lead beast had not attacked. Maybe it was waiting for the others. She had to work fast before the numbers were too great to overcome.

She pitched the stone to her left. As she hoped, the sound drew the invaders' attention in that direction. Back exposed, Gleenda darted forward. The invader had the strange weapon up near his face, pointing at the trees. He began to turn as she streaked closer. Glenda braced the spear with both hands and drove it through the invader's throat as he turned.

The invader's weapon cracked. He cried out and fell back. Writhing on the ground, blood spraying from his mouth, he wrapped his hands around the spear and tried to pull it free. Though stunned at what she had done, Gleenda dove, grabbed the spear and said, "Let me help you with that." She ripped it out. A gush of blood filled the hole. The man gagged.

The crack had drawn the attention of the other invaders. Many ran her way. A few made their weapons crack. She felt the heat on her body as the hot darts the weapons spit passed ever so close.

Gleenda raced into the shelter of the trees, then flew to the far left of the forest. With all attention diverted to the right, Gleenda dashed out and speared a second invader, this one in the back. The invader screamed and clutched at the spear. Gleenda shoved it in farther, but had trouble retracting it.

The invader dropped to his knees. As the others turned their way, Gleenda put both feet on the invader's back and pulled hard. The spear slid free. Again, she sped for the trees. This time, several more of the hot darts followed her.

From a high perch she watched as the other beasts pulled up in a line with the first. On a signal from the first rider, all four beasts moved forward.

"No!" Gleenda cried. The attack had begun and she could do nothing to stop the onslaught. No, she would not sit back and watch the annihilation of her homeland.

Targeting the same rider as before, Gleenda flew straight at him. The rider's eyes bulged, telling her she'd been seen. The large shovel on the beast's face rose to intercept her. The rider pointed at her, yelling a warning to the others. All eyes swung her way. Darts flew past. She was too fast and too small for them. She slid around the shovel and drove the spear deep into the rider's gut. He howled, swatted at her, then grabbed the spear with both hands. The beast ground to a halt.

Unable to withdraw the spear, Gleenda, clawed at the rider's face, leaving it bloody. She flew away. As she sped to safety, something ripped a hole through her left wing. The pain made her veer. She

missed flying headfirst into a tree by inches. The hole, though small, affected her ability to fly.

She reached a branch and settled to examine the damage. A toucan and a howler monkey were first to her side. Their concerned looks helped, but they could offer no assistance.

"I'm sorry, friends. I'm not sure how much more I can do. I have failed you."

The toucan took flight. The howler leapt to a lower branch and did what it was named for. It howled a warning to the forest. In the distance, its cries were picked up and relayed. The monkey ceased its warning abruptly. It looked down. Gleenda did the same. Below were three invaders, walking through the forest—*her* forest—with their weapons ready. *Were they hunting for her or anything that lived there?*

One of the invaders glanced up and spotted her. He shouted, pointed, then fired. The dart struck her leg and lifted her small body from her perch. The pain was intense. She managed to engage her wings before she hit the ground, but it only slowed her fall. The contact left her stunned and in more pain than she thought she could endure.

As the invaders closed on her, the howler overhead went berserk. Its cries filled the forest. One of the invaders fired at the howler to stop the noise. It only worked to intensify the warning tone of its voice.

The three invaders circled her. Gleenda believed her end had come. She looked into the eyes of one of the invaders. They did not show fear or hatred. Instead she saw, curiosity and wonder. They spoke in their strange language. After a few moments, one put his weapon away and bent to pick her up.

A poison dart tree frog leapt on his back. A second followed. The invader jumped and swatted at them. One fell and hopped away. A second invader smacked the other frog to the ground and stomped on it.

A spider monkey jumped down, snatched the weapon from the third invader's hands and scampered away. Two macaws dove and clipped the man who killed the tree frog, knocking him down. As soon as he landed, a massive anaconda curled around him. The invader's screams echoed through the trees.

The first man writhed on the ground as the poison from the tree frog took effect. The third weaponless invader panicked and ran. A group of ten howler monkeys dropped on him, tearing at his flesh with strong, nimble claws. His pain-filled cries joined with the other two in a symphony of the dying.

In a minute, the forest was silent.

Gleenda sat up. Blood seeped from the wound. Her body had a natural healing ability, but this wound was different. She suspected the dart was still in her. Her body may not know how to respond to the alien intrusion. Time would tell. For now, the forest denizens were ready to defend their homes. She had a battle to lead.

She floated off the forest floor and glanced around at the gathered creatures. A more diverse and determined army there had never been. "Let's take back our home," she said. The responding mixture of voices filled her with hope. She spotted a sheath on the belt of the poisoned man. He still writhed but offered no opposition to her taking the knife. Being almost one-third her body length, it was difficult to wield, but now she had a proper weapon to lead the fight.

They advanced toward the forest edge. The beasts were silent for the moment. Many invaders paced before the forest. All had weapons. They were ready for a fight.

A squad of howlers lifted their voices. The invaders stepped back. A few fired into the trees, but the sound of their weapons were lost amidst the high-pitched howls.

Gleenda flew forward. Her speed was slowed by the hole in her wing and the injury to her leg, but she was still fast enough to be on the beast rider before any defense could stop her. She slashed with the knife. It was heavy and unbalanced in her small hand, but she had the strength and rage to handle the weapon well enough to create a gout of blood from the rider's throat.

Gleenda didn't wait around to see what happened. She flew past, sliced at another invader standing on the ground, then made for the next beast.

All around her creatures charged. Darts flew from the defenders, dropping a handful of monkeys and a toucan, but the army was too vast. As a few of their companions were swarmed under, the invaders fell back.

Gleenda swooped in from behind and jabbed the blade into the rider's head. He slumped forward and did not move. She looked to the next one, but that rider had abandoned the beast and fled toward the camp they'd established.

"Onward, my friends," she shouted. "Chase the invaders from these lands."

A knot of invaders stood circled around the last beast. Its engine roared to life and the rider sent it toward the oncoming creatures. Some were caught and crushed under the massive weight. Other invaders kept up a steady barrage of their deadly darts. A path was carved through the ranks. What had once looked like a rout, now saw the tide turning.

Gleenda's hope faded. The beast spun around, chasing the creatures back toward the trees. If her team couldn't stop them now, all was lost, including their home.

Gleenda flew low to the ground, coming up behind the beast. Four invaders rode on top with the rider. Four others walked alongside. She slashed out, hamstringing one. He dropped to the ground. The man closest whirled and fired, driving Gleenda away. She was not able to find another opening to dart through.

The invaders closed to within ten feet of the trees. The denizen army was in full retreat. Then, from the right, bursting from the trees at lightning speed came the jungle's main predator, a massive muscle-lined jaguar. The invaders fled. The rider was caught before he got off the beast. The jaguar snapped its powerful jaw shut over the rider's face and his screams died in the creature's throat.

The sight of the jaguar inspired the army to give chase. A few invaders were caught. The ones that made camp hopped inside other beasts and sped off. In minutes, the battle for the forest was over. They had won.

As Gleenda hovered watching the invaders flee, she thought, *It's over. We won. We saved our home. For now.* But a knot deep in her stomach refused to ease. Her army had been lucky this time. The invaders would return, perhaps with a bigger army. Next time, that luck might not hold.

But for now, she was satisfied that at least there would be a next time.

Ocean Queen

NINE

Ocean Queen
Spirit of the Water

Her sleek muscular form slices through the deep sea water with ease. Her long yellow hair with the brown and white streaks flows back over her fine, bare blue shoulders. With a quick flip of her green-scaled tailfin, she makes a sharp change of direction. Her soft blue eyes are in constant motion, scanning the depths, not only for food, but to hunt out possible threats to the denizens of her underwater realm.

Too often her realm is threatened by invasion from the land walkers. Far too many of her kindred fish have been taken. And although that may be the circle of life, the quantity torn from the safety of the planet's waters has increased to near extinction of many species. It has to end, or at least slow to allow the replenishment of life.

Yet even that serious problem is not her main concern. It is the slow poisoning of the waters by the land walkers, endangering all life, not just beneath the waves, but eventually will affect them as well. They have to know, have to be aware they may be responsible for depleting an important food source. But that does not stop them from their constant pollution of such a valuable environment.

She searches for those responsible and metes out her own form of retribution for their crimes. But with so much water to patrol, catching the guilty before they add their poison is difficult.

A light draws her attention. It is deeper and moving away from her. Its course is straight. She pauses to watch, then, determining it is not a normal inhabitant of these depths, gives pursuit. Her tailfin pulses through the water, propelling her at great speed toward the intruder.

The vehicle levels off and slows. Its light is aimed downward, splitting the darkness in a white cone. She slows as she approaches, wanting to observe before she acts. So far, it has done nothing to warrant her quick and decisive punishment. She follows at a distance.

The land walker controlling the machine has not seen her, nor does she wish him to. To her knowledge, her kind is only a tall tale amongst the land walkers. She does not wish to prove the stories true. The only way she will make her presence known is if the land walker does something to endanger the water. Then it won't matter if she is seen, because the land walker will not be able to tell anyone. He will be lost at the bottom of the sea, never to be heard from again.

The light goes off. That surprises her. Usually, the land walkers cannot see at these depths without benefit of light. She moves closer, knowing without the light she is in little danger of discovery. She can see the vehicle. Her eyes are attuned to the darkness. Her vision cuts through the darkness with ease.

She recognizes the pilot of the craft as a land walker male. Judging by his mannerisms, he appears to be in distress. She closes on the vehicle and watches his face. He is working with frantic motions at restarting the machine. She notes it is sinking lower. This is not a good place to go down. The depths reach a distance even she doesn't like to venture. The pressures on her body could do permanent damage.

She swims to a position in front and a little above the glass where she can see the man and stay out of the machine's downward path. The man's face is moist. He perspires, but even more, he cries. He knows his end is imminent. As his hands fly across the console pushing various buttons, he is speaking to someone she cannot see. Whoever it is cannot give assistance.

The man glances up, perhaps catching her movement in his periphery. He freezes and for a moment, he forgets his problem. The anxiety fades from his face and a look of awe replaces it. They lock eyes. The man's are sorrowful yet filled with wonder. She knows nothing of this man, nor of his intent, but she has a feeling about him, one she cannot explain. She doesn't believe the man means her home harm.

His features are kind. His watery eyes warm. She knows nothing of him yet is surprised to realize she likes him. Like may not be the proper term. She is curious about him and wishes she knew his intentions toward her world.

As the machine plummets past her moving ever deeper, she makes a hasty decision. She dives after the ship using all her powerful muscles to pound at the water. She gains and overtakes the machine, but the pressure makes it difficult to breathe. She cannot go much farther or she will perish.

With a final push, she passes the vessel and turns into its path. Using her tail to brace, she absorbs the impact. The force drives her deeper. Her strength wanes, but she persists in her efforts. The machine slows, but not enough. She can no longer handle the pain. The pressure is too much.

With her last remnants of strength, she pushes up and to the side. The machine is sluggish to alter its course but does move. In slow degrees, it angles sideways then upward. As the fathoms lessen, so does the strain on her frame. She gains speed and is soon transporting the vessel upward at a greater speed than its descent.

With the force needed to travel much easier, she is able to pull back from the glass bubble. She sees him then, watching her. Tears still moisten his face, but the eyes no longer show fear. She sees warmth, perhaps gratitude.

She scans his face as he does hers. She has seen other land walkers, even had interactions with a few, though most not to the benefit of the walker. This one is different. She knows not why, but she senses the man's intentions are not malicious. She does not believe he is there to harm the water or the beings residing there. Perhaps some good land walkers do exist.

The water grows lighter as she nears the surface. She sees the shadow of the ship this smaller vessel originated from. The sunlight penetrates and she can make out more details of the man inside the machine. His features are soft and appealing. His hair is short and of a darker, similar color to hers. He is long and muscular; not as muscular as she, but not bad for a land walker.

But it is the eyes, the color of the water at this depth, that catches and holds her attention. So much is conveyed there. Warmth, gratefulness, joy. Perhaps regret; maybe even love. She is happy with her decision to save the walker.

He places a large hand on the glass and mouths something. She guesses, 'Thank you,' but doesn't know for sure. She will go with that, as it will enhance her memory of this encounter.

On a whim, she lifts one webbed hand from the machine and matches it with his. They are of a like size, except his hand has no webbing. She finds herself wishing she could communicate with this man. To learn more about him and his purpose in her home, but it is not to be. She will never give up her beautiful form to walk the land, even for a chance to meet and learn more about this land walker.

The machine breaks the surface, and she guides the vessel toward the larger one, keeping her body beneath the water and her head behind the glass bubble. She has shown herself to this walker but has no desire to do so to others.

A cacophony of noises greets her as the larger vessel moves toward the machine and those aboard shout in their language. The sea is so much quieter and peaceful below the surface.

The walker inside the machine presses both hands together, repeats the thank you, then does something strange. He places his fingers to his lips, then presses the fingers to the glass. A curious thing, but not one she understands.

She gives the machine one final shove and stays back. As the machine drifts toward the bigger one, the man waves. That is a gesture she understands. With a wave back, she dives for the depths with a hope that one day, the land walkers will come to understand the damage they do to her world and take measures to stop. If not, it will be up to her and her people to stop them.

She hopes that time never comes.

Angel of Peace

TEN

Angel of Peace

(I realize this artwork already appears, but I wrote this story before I discovered I'd already written the other one. I decided tom include it anyway.)

Rainbow

We are a people of colors. Bright, vivid, and warm, or dark, bold, and harsh. We run a full spectrum. As individuals we run the gamut of our own personal hues on a daily, sometimes hourly basis. We may feel dark and hostile in the morning and light and airy in the evening. Each emotion has its own designated shade. Our mood determines our colors. We are not limited in our range.

Understanding what colors make up our lives helps us understand our moods. They help us perceive the world and those around us. The colors lighten when faced with individuals or places that make you feel happy. Your spirit brightens, as do the colors you've assigned. In contrast, when placed in a hostile environment or meeting those who anger you, bring forth negative memories, or threaten you, the colors are deep, dark, and angry.

Knowing who we are makes our lives much easier and happier. That we have the ability to be a multitude of colors should allow us to understand and accept that as a people we are those same colors.

How can we judge others for their beliefs, preferences, or choices in how they live their lives when we share those same hues? Because we may prefer blue instead of green does not mean we don't appreciate a rainbow when we see one.

Take the time to discover your rainbow. Then understand we each have our own version.

Other Titles

Random Survival Series
Random Survival
The Long Search For Home
The Endless Struggle
The Journey to Normal
Then There'll Be None

Danny Roth Series
Teammates
Teamwork
Home Team
Stealing Home
Group Therapy
Double Play

The Dead Series
Tower of the Dead
Island of the Dead
Escaping the Dead

Pick-A-Path Series
Pick-A-Path: Apocalypse 1
Pick-A-Path: Apocalypse 2
Pick-A-Path: Apocalypse 3

Stand Alone Titles

Warriors of the Court   The Eliminator   Ghost of a Chance
Live to Die Again   Mischief Magic

Short Stories

The Con   Short Stop-A Danny Roth short
Super Me   Super Me Too

Co-authored with Jason J. Nugent

Escape: The Seam Travelers Book 1

Capture: The Seam Travelers Book 2

Conquest: The Seam Travelers Book 3